Molly

Based on *The Railway Series* by the Rev. W. Awdry

Illustrations by
Robin Davies and Jerry Smith

EGMONT

EGMONT

We bring stories to life

First published in Great Britain in 2006
by Egmont UK Limited
239 Kensington High Street, London W8 6SA
This edition published in 2008
All Rights Reserved

HiT entertainment

ISBN 978 1 4052 3487 0
1 3 5 7 9 10 8 6 4 2
Printed in Italy

The Forest Stewardship Council (FSC) is an international, non-governmental organisation dedicated to promoting responsible management of the world's forests. FSC operates a system of forest certification and product labelling that allows consumers to identify wood and wood-based products from well managed forests.

For more information about Egmont's paper buying policy please visit www.egmont.co.uk/ethicalpublishing

For more information about the FSC please visit their website at www.fsc.uk.org

This is a story about Molly, a bright yellow engine. Molly didn't think she was very special because she only pulled empty trucks. But one night Molly realised just how useful she was . . .

It was a blustery evening on the Island of Sodor. Thomas was passing through one of his favourite stations.

"Toot, toot!" called Thomas to the Stationmaster. Thomas liked this station because every evening the Stationmaster put up lots of lanterns all along the platform.

But Thomas was also busy thinking about the next day. "I wonder what Molly, the new engine, will be like?" he chuffed.

When Thomas pulled into Brendam Docks the next morning, he spotted Molly straight away. She was waiting in a siding looking very sad.

"What's the matter?" puffed Thomas.

"Emily made fun of me because I have to take empty trucks to the Coaling Plant," replied Molly, sadly.

Just then, the signal turned to red. Gordon thundered past with the Express. "You wait there," he chuffed. "My Express is more important than your empty trucks!"

Molly chugged off very sadly.

As Thomas wondered what he could do, the wind blew over some containers covered in tarpaulin. The tarpaulin began to rustle.

"That's it!" puffed Thomas, happily, and raced off to find Molly.

With the help of Molly's Driver, Thomas and Molly covered her trucks with the tarpaulin.

"With your trucks covered no one will know they are empty," explained Thomas. "We'll make them think you are carrying a very special delivery!"

Thomas spent a busy day telling everyone about Molly's special.

Percy and Edward were talking to Thomas in Knapford Station when Gordon pulled in.

"I don't care what you say, Thomas," puffed Gordon. "Nothing can be as important as my Express."

"It can," chugged Thomas angrily. "Be at Abbey Station tonight and you will see just how special Molly's special is!"

As the engines pulled away, Thomas realised what he had said.

"How am I going to make Molly's special even more special?" Thomas chuffed, thoughtfully. He pulled into his favourite station just as the Stationmaster was lighting his lanterns. This gave Thomas another idea.

"Can I borrow your lanterns?" he puffed. Although the Stationmaster was a little curious he was happy to lend Thomas his lanterns. Thomas loaded up his trucks and sped off.

That evening, Molly waited for Thomas at the Coaling Plant.

"Hello, Molly," puffed Thomas, happily. "I have had another idea about how to make your special even more special!" And Thomas told Molly all about his plan.

Very soon, Molly was covered in lanterns and heading happily for Abbey Station.

"Toot, toot!" whistled Percy and Emily, as Molly arrived at the station.

"I feel very special," chuffed Molly, with a big smile on her face. "Thank you, Thomas."

Suddenly, a big gust of wind blew right through the station. It lifted the tarpaulin covering Molly's empty trucks and blew out the lanterns! Everyone could see that there was nothing underneath.

"I knew your trucks couldn't be as important as my Express!" chuffed Gordon, smiling.

Molly screeched out of the station. She wanted to be as far away from all the other engines as possible.

"Well," chuffed Emily. "What are you going to do now, Thomas? Poor Molly, you have just made her look very silly."

"Thomas," the Stationmaster called across the platform. "Where's Molly? The Fat Controller has just phoned. There are engines waiting at the Coaling Plant. They need Molly's empty trucks so they can deliver the coal!"

Thomas raced out of the yard looking for Molly. He went all round the Island. Eventually he found Molly stopped in a siding.

"I'm very sorry," apologised Thomas. "But I have some really good news," he chuffed, merrily. "Your empty trucks are very important! They need them at the Coaling Plant right now."

"But I've nearly run out of coal," sobbed Molly, more upset than before.

"Don't worry," chuffed Thomas. "I'll help you."

"OK, Thomas, you push and I'll pull," puffed Molly. Very soon the two engines were working together to get Molly and her empty trucks to the Coaling Plant.

The Coaling Plant engines were very glad to see Molly and her empty trucks.

"Quick, quick," they chugged. "We need to start our deliveries and we need your empty trucks to carry the coal."

"Look how important your trucks are!" puffed Thomas.

Molly looked around at her trucks being used to help the Coaling Plant engines and thought how special an engine she was. She was so proud it made her axles tingle!

"More trucks, more trucks," called out Henry, one of the Coaling Plant engines.

Without a moment's thought, Molly rushed past Thomas, whistling, "I'll get more trucks!" Molly couldn't wait to begin pulling empty trucks again.

"And I'll help," puffed Thomas. Molly and Thomas raced back to the yard to pick up some more trucks.

Just as they were leaving the yard with their empty trucks, the signal turned to red. But this time Gordon and his Express had to wait.

"Out of the way!" puffed Molly. "Empty trucks coming through!"

"You see," laughed Thomas. "Sometimes empty trucks are more important than your Express!"

Molly felt even more special. Now she knew what it was like to be a Really Useful Engine. She was never going to feel bad about pulling empty trucks again.

The Thomas Story Library is THE definitive collection of stories about Thomas and ALL his friends.

5 more Thomas Story Library titles will be chuffing into your local bookshop in August 2008!

Jeremy
Hector
BoCo
Billy
Whiff

And there are even more Thomas Story Library books to follow la

So go on, start your Thomas Story Library NOW!

A Fantastic Offer for Thomas the Tank Engine Fans!

STICK
POUND
COIN
HERE

In every Thomas Story Library book like this one, you will find a special token. Collect 6 Thomas tokens and we will send you a brilliant Thomas poster, and a double-sided bedroom door hanger! Simply tape a £1 coin in the space above, and fill out the form overleaf.

TO BE COMPLETED BY AN ADULT

To apply for this great offer, ask an adult to complete the coupon below and send it with a pound coin and 6 tokens, to:
THOMAS OFFERS, PO BOX 715, HORSHAM RH12 5WG

☐ Please send a Thomas poster and door hanger. I enclose 6 tokens plus a £1 coin. (Price includes P&P)

Fan's name...

Address...

....Postcode.............................

Date of birth..

Name of parent/guardian...

Signature of parent/guardian..